W9-BZS-254

DATE DUE

Opening Night

by

Rachel Isadora

GREENWILLOW BOOKS · NEW YORK

WELCOME GILLIAN

Library of Congress Cataloging in Publication Data

Isadora, Rachel.   Opening night.
Summary: Heather, a young ballerina, experiences
the off-stage and on-stage excitement of
opening night at the ballet.
[1. Ballet dancing—Fiction]   I. Title.
PZ7.I7630p   1984   [E]   83-20791
ISBN 0-688-02726-1
ISBN 0-688-02727-X (lib. bdg.)

"Hurry, hurry," Heather says.
"We mustn't be late."

"Don't worry," says her mother.
"We have plenty of time. The house
lights are just going on."

Backstage is filled with flowers.
"All ready for opening night?" Sam, the guard, asks.
"Yes, I am," Heather replies.

Heather is too impatient to wait for the elevator.
She runs up the stairs. The third floor is crowded
with trunks and crates. The usually dim halls are
brightly lit. Everything looks different.

Music drifts from a rehearsal room.
Heather peeks in and sees one of the
ballerinas warming up.

At the end of the hall is Laura's dressing room.
She is Heather's favorite ballerina. Heather knocks at
the door, but there is no answer. She takes a package
out of her bag and places it in front of the door.
Then she hurries to the children's dressing room.

Heather's mother and her friend Libby are already
there. "Hi, Heather. I saved a place for you next
to me," Libby says. Heather turns on the lights
around her mirror.
"Just like a star," her mother says, smiling.

"If we hurry we can go to the canteen," Libby says.
"Maybe Laura will be there," Heather says hopefully.
"No, she won't," Libby replies. "She's probably resting."

   Libby giggles. "There's Bottom. He's so funny."
"Look at those tutus. I wish our costumes had tutus,"
  Heather says.
"Don't be silly. Bugs never wear tutus," Libby announces.
"We better get back."

They dance their way
to the dressing room.

Heather puts on her bathrobe. She hums the music to her part.
Suddenly she's nervous. Her hands feel cold and clammy.
"Remember to keep your knees straight, remember to keep your
knees straight," she repeats to herself.

"You're first, Heather," Pete, the makeup man, says.
He puts rouge on her cheeks, lipstick on her lips,
and dabs glitter on her eyelids.

"Now I really look like Laura,"
Heather says.

In the costume room Heather changes quickly.
She clips on her antennae and stands on point.

"Remember," the wardrobe mistress warns,
"no sitting once you have your costume on."

"Five minutes to curtain. On stage everyone!"
the loudspeaker booms.

The stagehands are making
last-minute changes.

"How's the weather up there, Al?"
a voice calls to a stagehand
fixing the moon.

The lights grow dim. There is a hush backstage.
Heather hears the audience applaud.
The overture begins and the curtain rises.

"Stand back in the wings," cautions the ballet mistress.
"If you see the audience, they can see you."
"Listen for your cue," the stage manager says.

The music swells.
"Here we go," says the lead bug.

It is time for Heather's solo.
She takes a deep breath.
She turns, jumps, and flies.

The audience applauds.

Laura, the Fairy Queen, waves her wand
and the bugs dance quickly off stage.
But the excitement isn't over.
In the wings the bugs jump up and down.

"You were great," Libby tells Heather.
"Shhsh!" the stage manager orders. "The ballet
  is still on." In a quiet group the bugs watch the end
  of the performance.

"Everyone on stage for bows!" The bugs hold hands
as they take their places. The curtain rises.

"I can't see anyone. It's so dark," Heather whispers.
"Keep smiling, they can see you," a ballerina cautions her.
"Bravo, bravo!" cries the audience.

After the final curtain Laura goes over to Heather
and gives her a kiss. "Thank you for the leg warmers.
It must have taken you a long time to knit them.
I'll wear them for good luck."

When the bugs return to the dressing room,
there is a surprise waiting for them—
a bouquet of roses at each place.

"See you tomorrow, bug," Libby says.
"Good night, bug," says Heather.